THE SAILOR'S BOOK

by Charlotte Agell

FIREFLY BOOKS

Canadian Cataloguing in Publication Data
Agell, Charlotte, 1959–
    The sailor's book

ISBN 0-920668-90-9 (bound)
ISBN 0-920668-91-7 (pbk.)

I. Title.

PZ7.A34Sa 1991   j813′.54   C91-094437-7

A FIREFLY BOOK

Published by
Firefly Books Ltd.
250 Sparks Ave.,
Willowdale, Ontario
Canada   M2H 2S4

Design: Michael Solomon
Printed and bound in Canada

The sun

is a dragon's eye.

Clouds

are a dragon's breath.

Waves

are the scales
on a dragon's back.

I am the captain
of my own boat

and you
are the captain of yours.

Together we sail
on the dragon's back

catching his breath
in our sails

and tickling his scales.

The wind is his laugh,
a gentle evening breeze.

Red sky at night,
sailor's delight.

We race to the opposite shore,
as the dragon softly snores.

A squall blows in
whenever he sneezes.

This is a dragon
who does what he pleases!

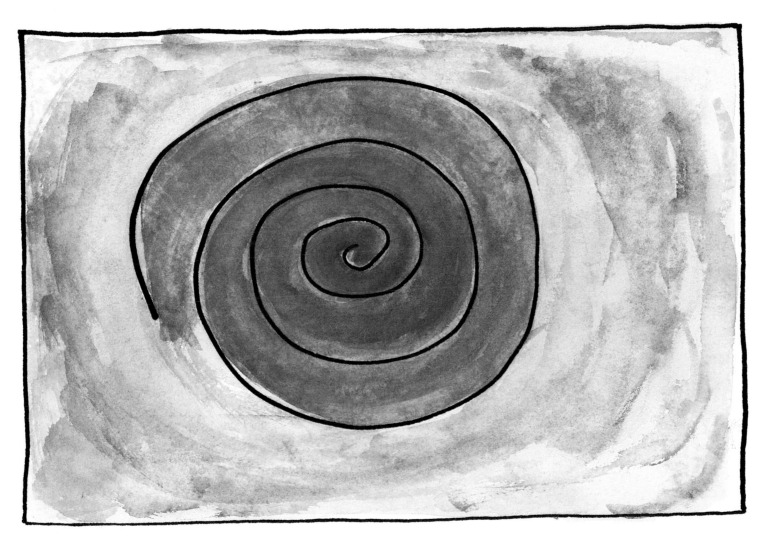

Red sky at morning

sailor, take warning!

The dragon is angry
and brewing a storm.

He shakes his back
and the waves grow wilder.

He opens his mouth
and the gale winds roar.

Quick, reef the mainsail!
Haul in the jib!

And sail, one and all,
to a quiet cove

far from the storm
where the wild winds won't blow.

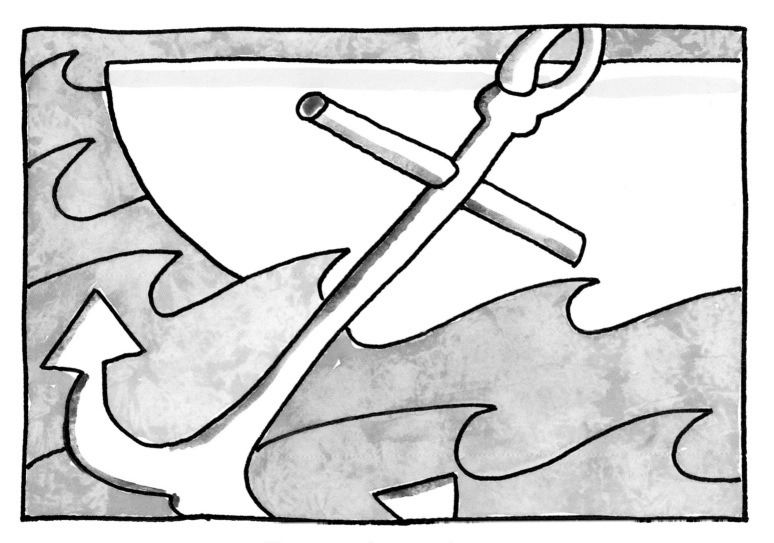

Here, we drop anchor
to rest from adventure.

We drink lemonade
as we watch the storm fade.

The dragon yawns and is calm,
his ancient eye winks.

There's a red sky tonight
and each of us thinks

tomorrow will be fine
for sailing.